T0145056

Rose Boston's JOURNEY

Thelma V. Crump

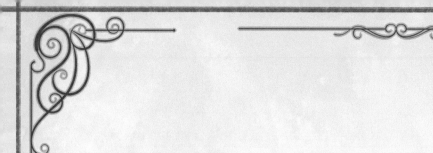

Archway Publishing books may be ordered through booksellers or by contacting:

Archway Publishing
1663 Liberty Drive
Bloomington, IN 47403
www.archwaypublishing.com
844-669-3957

ISBN: 978-1-6657-4729-5 (sc)
ISBN: 978-1-6657-5118-6 (hc)
ISBN: 978-1-6657-4728-8 (e)

Print information available on the last page.

Archway Publishing rev. date: 09/21/2023

ARCHWAY
PUBLISHING

To all that believe in the power of love.

I dedicate this book in memory to my beautiful grandmothers, Mrs. Rosetta Gardner Crump, and Mrs. Elizabeth Nickerson McCoy Simmons.

I also dedicate this book to the strength and resilience of my Aunt, Mrs. Jessie Simmons Alexander, and my mother, Mrs. Edith Pauline Young Crump.

To Anthony, my rock.

Rose is 25 years old and has obtained her education to become America's first black veterinarian. After attending a social in the big city of Atlantis to raise awareness on animal issues, she and two friends start their journey 200 miles by car back to Tallavese. A car approaching their car loses control. The driver of Rose's car is knocked unconscious, and Rose grabs the wheel. The car spins and flips, causing Rose to be thrown from the car and clinging for life.

They are all rushed to the hospital in Atlantis and while the other two car companions are treated for minor cuts and bruises, Rose is treated for shock, a crushed right hand and broken ribs. "I don't know what happened," she says while lying in shock on the gurney as the doctor makes his diagnosis. "All I know is that we were happy, talking about the social, the future and then all of a sudden a car comes out of nowhere and hits us!"

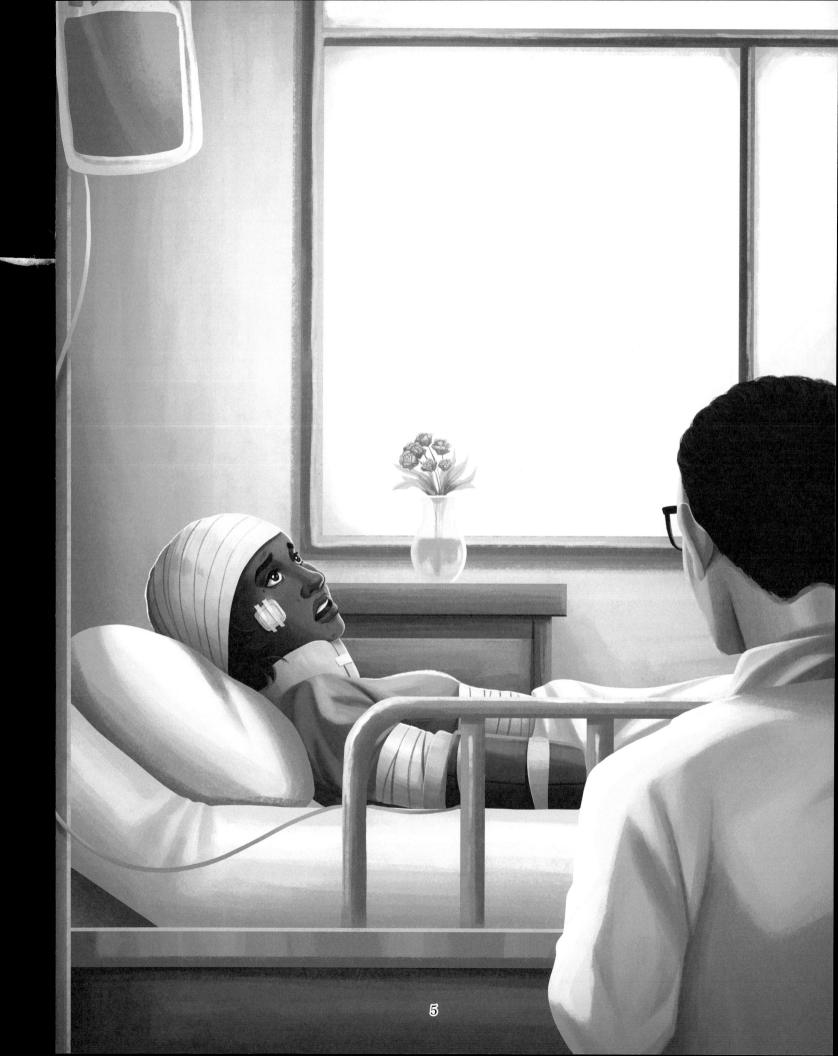

Rose's parents are called and they take a train to Atlantis. They are informed by the doctor that Rose will be fine, but she has suffered broken ribs and her hand was so severely crushed that he feared the worse – she would never use it again. Mama Boston immediately cries out at the doctor that her daughter has and will have the will to use her hand again and is planning a career as a veterinarian. "She just graduated – she has her whole life and career ahead of her!" Mama Boston shouted. "Please don't take that away from her!" The doctor informed Mama and Papa Boston that he had told Rose of her condition and that she was in a state of depression. Mama and Papa Boston ask to see Rose.

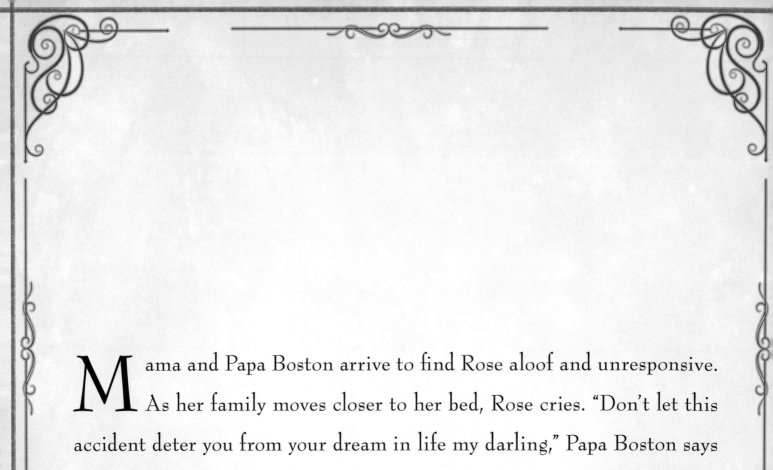

Mama and Papa Boston arrive to find Rose aloof and unresponsive. As her family moves closer to her bed, Rose cries. "Don't let this accident deter you from your dream in life my darling," Papa Boston says to Rose. "You must build on this as a challenge to regain your strength and passion for what you love most – and that is to become a veterinarian and help educate others to follow in your footsteps." "I am afraid I won't be able to Papa," Rose says to her father and mother. "The doctor has said that I won't be able to use my hand again – my hand is crushed!" She cries uncontrollably. Her parents console her.

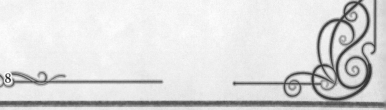

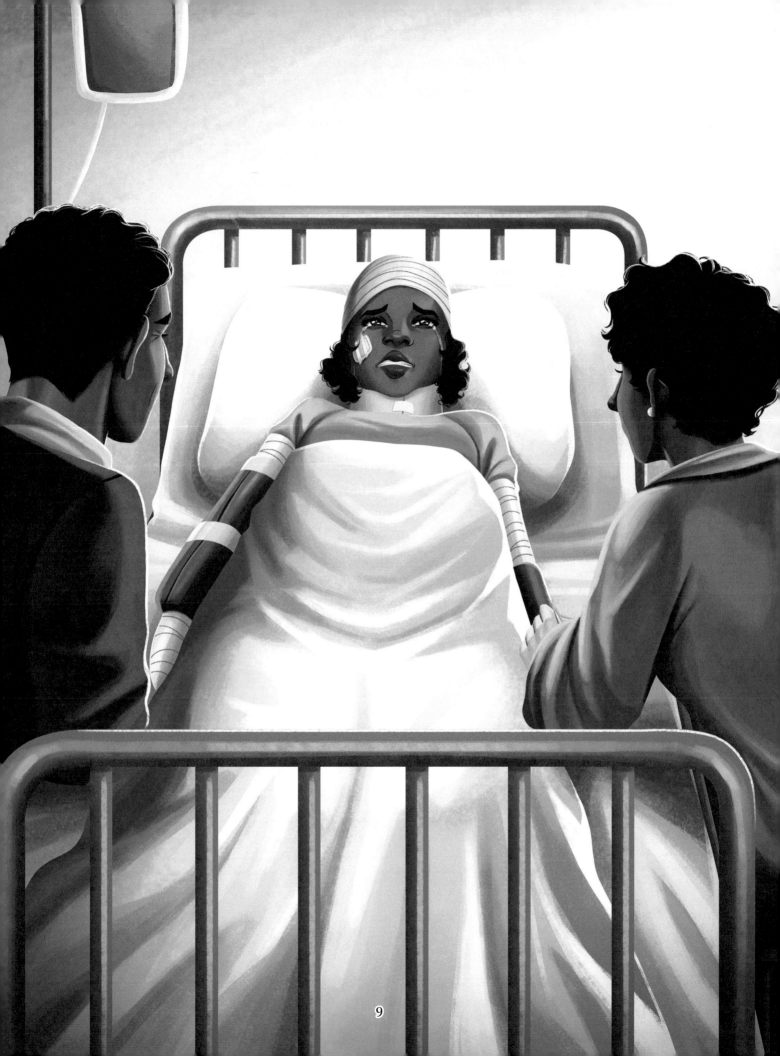

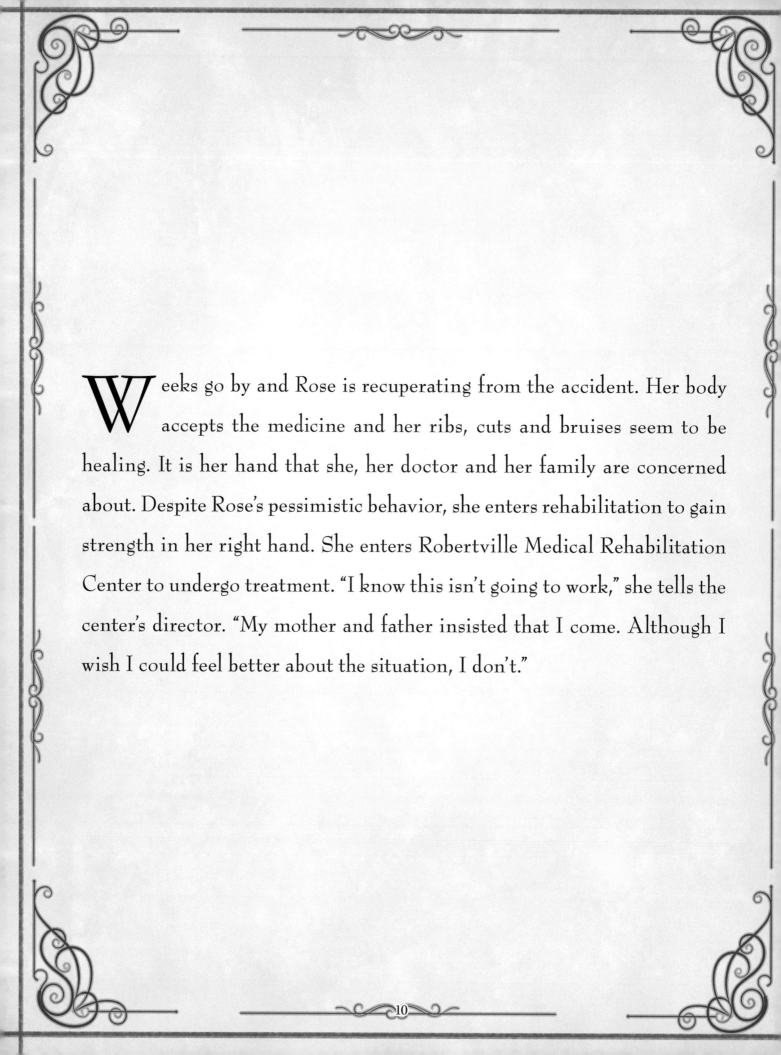

Weeks go by and Rose is recuperating from the accident. Her body accepts the medicine and her ribs, cuts and bruises seem to be healing. It is her hand that she, her doctor and her family are concerned about. Despite Rose's pessimistic behavior, she enters rehabilitation to gain strength in her right hand. She enters Robertville Medical Rehabilitation Center to undergo treatment. "I know this isn't going to work," she tells the center's director. "My mother and father insisted that I come. Although I wish I could feel better about the situation, I don't."

While at Robertville, Rose sees an old friend, Jack Holbrook. Jack was at Robertville visiting a relative and he walks over to Rose to say hello. Rose tells Jack about her situation, and he tells her he had heard about it in Tallavese. "I often think about you and especially now with the accident and all .....," he tells Rose. "Your parents told my parents about your situation, and all I could do is wonder how you were doing and is there anything I could do to help." "You are so kind and I appreciate the offer, but I am doing well," said Rose. "I feel there are so many obstacles, and I won't be able to use my right hand again – never ever!" Jack tells Rose she should not use "can't" or "never ever" in her vocabulary again. "Things happen for a reason Rose," said Jack. "You mustn't let this stop you from your life-long dream of becoming a veterinarian. I've seen you with animals and you adore them. You have so much to offer to the world and it still can be done."

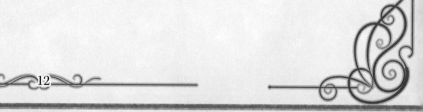

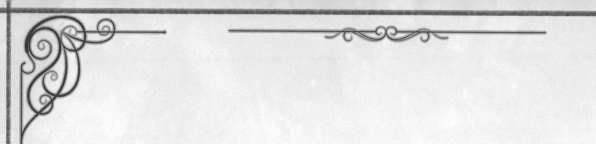

Rose fires back at Jack by saying he is not the one with the handicap. He asks her if she's tried the rehabilitation. She says to a certain degree, but adds, "It's not going to do any good." Jack immediately picks up one of Rose's exercise devices and helps her with it. "With timing and good will and grace you will overcome this handicap and become the first African American veterinarian. Others will learn from you and you will set the standard," he tells Rose. "You must enjoy your journey and by doing so, you will need patience, and optimism.

As time goes on, Rose begins to use the equipment at Robertville and movement in her hand begins to occur. Later, she is able to write her name again. During this time, Jack comes by on a regular basis to assist Rose in her rehabilitation, and she and Jack grow closer. Mama and Papa Boston see improvement in their daughter's behavior and willingness and her affectionately growing attachment to Jack.

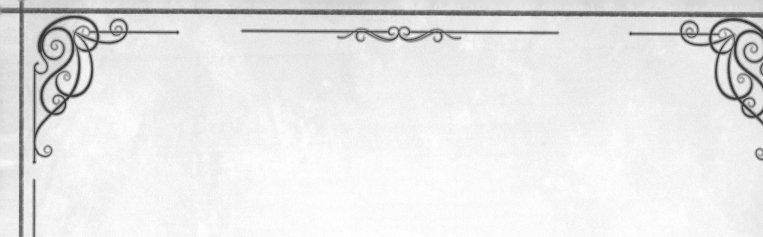

Soon Rose is strong enough to consider her work as a veterinarian. Although her doctor didn't have much hope for Rose to have a full recovery, he sees nothing short of a miracle. Rose's doctor tells her how far she has come, and she has defied most obstacles to lead a successful life as a veterinarian. "You have proven me wrong Rose, and I applaud you for this," he said. "Persevere and continue to stay focused and strong willed." Rose smiles, but in the back of her mind wonders if she will be able to practice medicine due to her injured hand.

Within weeks, Rose is discharged from Robertville. She is at home and receives a call from a veterinarian clinic in Atlantis that wishes to hire her as a veterinarian based on her past accolades and abilities. She tells the caller she is not sure she is interested and hangs up the phone.

Mama Boston overhears her conversation with the caller from the clinic. "Rose darling, how do you know if you don't try?" You are missing out on opportunity of a lifetime — something you have dreamed about since you were a child." Rose replies, "Mama, it's not that simple. I am afraid of the unknown, the future, failure. What if I fail?" Mama Boston quickly replies to her daughter in a loving and nurturing way, "My darling little angel, as long as you stay positive about your life, you will never fail. You have the abilities, the passion and the imagination to achieve your dream. Trust in God and you will be just fine. Trust in yourself."

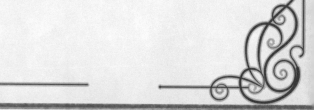

Rose picks up a scalpel she used in veterinarian school and begins to think. She calls Jack. She tells Jack that she would like for him to accompany her to Atlantis for a visit to the veterinarian clinic. He agrees without hesitation. Rose calls the veterinarian clinic and asks if she can come for a visit. They tell her yes.

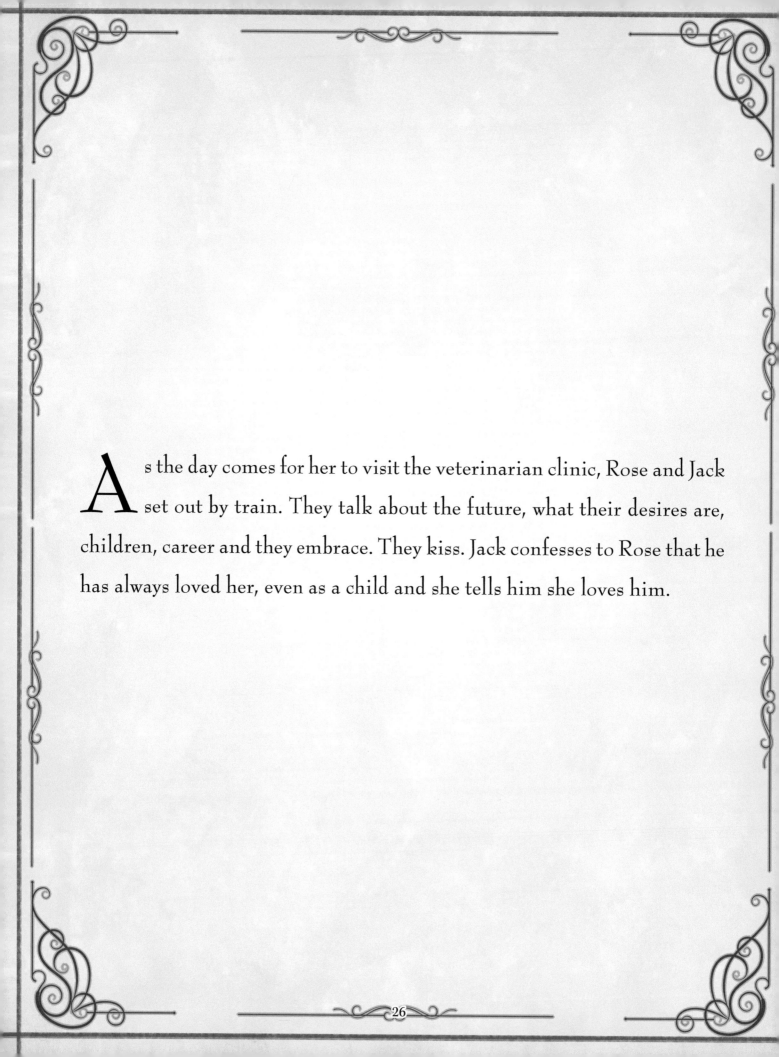

As the day comes for her to visit the veterinarian clinic, Rose and Jack set out by train. They talk about the future, what their desires are, children, career and they embrace. They kiss. Jack confesses to Rose that he has always loved her, even as a child and she tells him she loves him.

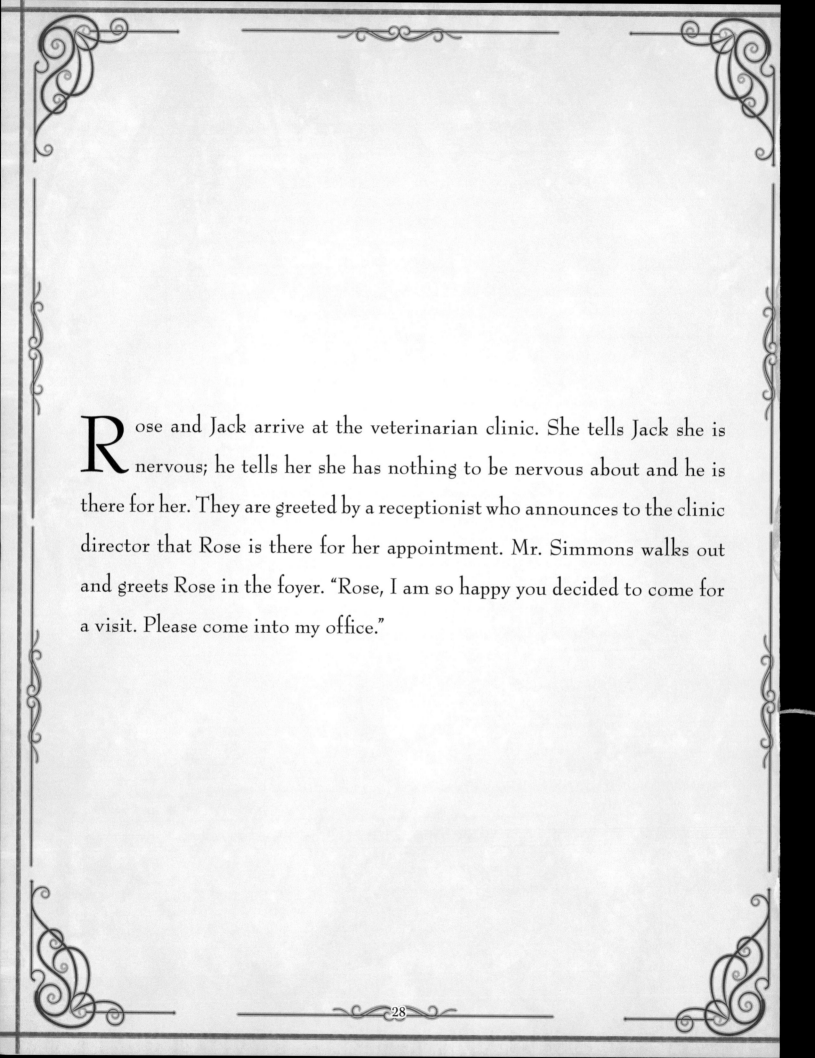

Rose and Jack arrive at the veterinarian clinic. She tells Jack she is nervous; he tells her she has nothing to be nervous about and he is there for her. They are greeted by a receptionist who announces to the clinic director that Rose is there for her appointment. Mr. Simmons walks out and greets Rose in the foyer. "Rose, I am so happy you decided to come for a visit. Please come into my office."

As Rose walks away she lets go of Jack's hand. Jack tells Rose, "I am here for you. Remember, you must enjoy your journey."

Rose and Mr. Simmons talk and Jack waits nervously outside of his office. Forty-five minutes later, Rose exits Mr. Simmons' office and she shakes his hand. "Thank you again for the opportunity to come and visit with you and your clinic, Mr. Simmons," said Rose.

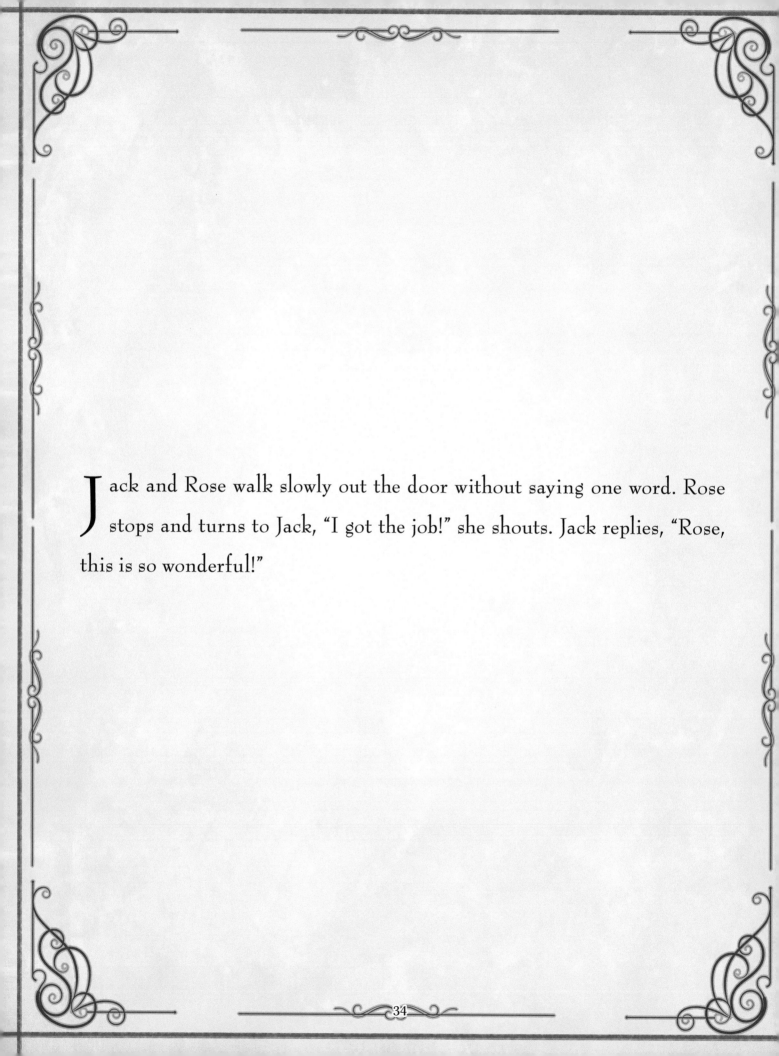

Jack and Rose walk slowly out the door without saying one word. Rose stops and turns to Jack, "I got the job!" she shouts. Jack replies, "Rose, this is so wonderful!"

They embrace and cry. "I knew you could do it Rose, you just had to have faith in yourself!" "I know Jack, and I couldn't have done it without you!" "I had to show him I could use my hands to perform operations and I did it!" They rush to the station to catch their train back to Tallavese.

Rose Boston became the first black veterinarian and later became an instructor at the School of Veterinarian Medicine in a well-established university in the south.

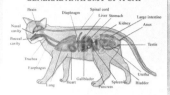

GENERAL ANATOMY OF A CAT

Two years after her visit to Mr. Simmons at the clinic, Rose married Jack Holbrook in a beautiful southern church wedding in Tallavese.

They became the proud parents of three beautiful children. They live on a 400 acre estate where Jack is a successful businessman, rancher and cattleman. Rose continued her work as a veterinarian and opened the first animal hospital in Tallavese.

Printed in the United States
by Baker & Taylor Publisher Services